To Becky
on your 6th Birthday
Love Jessica

This 1995 edition published by Derrydale Books,
distributed by Random House Value Publishing, Inc.,
40 Engelhard Avenue, Avenel, New Jersey 07001
© 1994 Jane Wardle and Georgina Hargreaves.
Produced by Emma Books Ltd., Beckington, Somerset, U.K.
Illustrated by Georgina Hargreaves. Printed in Italy.
A CIP Catalog Record for this book is available from the Library of Congress.
ISBN 0-517-12064-X

Random House
New York • Toronto • London • Sydney • Auckland

Prince Brownie's Rescue

Written by Jane Wardle
Illustrated by Georgina Hargreaves

DERRYDALE BOOKS
NEW YORK • AVENEL

Every year Mrs. Watson, the owner of Tanpit riding stables, visited the local Pony Market. This year, as she wandered between pens of ponies herded from the fields, she looked for suitable ponies to take local children safely on rides.

The loud speaker announced the start of the sale in the main arena, so Mrs. Watson quickly found herself a seat at the ringside.

Pony after pony entered the sandy arena and was sold. Heads nodded, hands were raised and the auctioneer shouted, "Going, going, gone!" in a loud voice, and banged his hammer down on to the hard wood.

Mrs. Watson bought two ponies, a grey and a little piebald, and quickly thought of names for them. She would call them Smokey and Jigsaw.

7

As the sale came to an end, Mrs. Watson paid for the ponies and after much pushing and shoving, loaded them into the horsetrailer. There was space for just one more pony. She decided to take a look around the market to see if she had missed anything.

The afternoon light was beginning to fade as she turned the corner to see a very grubby, grumpy looking pony, but there was something about him that attracted her.

He was quite unsuitable for her riding stables and flattened his ears and tried to bite her every time she went near him. He even turned his back as if to kick her. He was painfully thin with long scars across his back and neck, and one of his front hooves had a crack running down the middle of it. His mane and tail were long and matted, but he held his head high and under his dull brown coat was a beautifully shaped body.

"Is this pony sold?" Mrs. Watson asked the rather meanlooking man who seemed to be in charge of him. The man's face lit up as he said, "Not yet, my dear. He's a real bargain though."

Mrs. Watson had a daughter called Ruth who competed in county shows. She wondered if this pony could be a good show pony for her, but she was still not quite sure.

"Well if you can get him into my horsetrailer, I'll take him," she said.

Even though the pony was painfully weak, he walked up the ramp of the box with complete confidence. When the horsetrailer arrived home, Mrs. Watson stayed for a while looking over the stable door at the grumpy brown pony.

"I will call you Prince Brownie, because you are as proud and as haughty as a prince," she told him.

The next day was Saturday and the yard was filled with children dressed in jodphurs, excitedly wondering which horse they would ride this week.

Jane had come to the stables early to help Mrs. Watson groom and tack up the ponies. She was a fairly tall girl with long brown hair and large, blue eyes.

After the ponies had set off on their ride, Jane went around to Prince Brownie's stable to help Mrs. Watson muck it out. "He's beautiful," said Jane as she gazed at the skinny brown pony.

"Well, he will be!" replied Mrs. Watson leaning on her fork and looking at the pony. "He's not really nasty, he has been mistreated and only bites and makes faces because he does not trust us yet. He needs a lot of care and attention. I am sure he will be much happier then."

"If only Prince Brownie were mine," thought Jane, "I would make him well and take care of him forever."

That night Jane told her mother all about the new pony and
how wonderful he was - and how she was going to help
Mrs. Watson make him well by feeding him lots of oats.
"Would you like me to make him some oatmeal?"
asked Jane's mother. "Not those sort of oats," said Jane,
"You don't feed oatmeal to a pony."

The next day Prince Brownie was put in a paddock of his own. He greedily ate fresh grass, desperate to fill his belly. After a few weeks, the pony's strength grew and he put on weight. Instead of being barely able to walk up the hill to the paddock, he would canter around, neighing to the ponies in the field on the other side of the hedge.

One day, when Mrs. Watson and Jane led him through the gateway of his field and released him, Prince Brownie cantered away and skidded to a halt facing the hedge. Several times he cantered up to the hedge, stopped, turned away and cantered up to it again.

"What is he doing?" Jane asked in a puzzled tone.

The third time, instead of stopping, he cantered faster, lifted up his front legs and jumped the high hedge! Mrs. Watson and Jane could hardly believe their eyes, but they knew immediately what a very special pony he must be. "That's the best jumping pony I have ever seen," said Mrs. Watson.

"I don't think that Prince Brownie will ever be mine now," thought Jane, "Mrs. Watson would never sell a pony as good as that."

It was not long before Prince Brownie was completely healthy. He was full of life and spirit. His coat shone like polished mahogany covered in highlights and his black eyes glinted with mischief. He still nipped at any stray hand which tried to stroke his silky neck over the stable door. He was treated with the utmost respect by the children.

The better Prince Brownie became, the more he needed to occupy his mind. He was very easily bored. Left alone in his stable, he would cause all kinds of trouble. He would kick his water buckets over and pull his hayrack down. If he ate his corn from a bucket, he would spray his feed everywhere. When he was finished, he would pick up the bucket between his teeth, shaking it so that the bucket would be thrown through the open top door of his stable. After breaking several buckets he was given a heavy trough in the corner of his stable from which to eat.

At last Mrs. Watson's daughter was ready to take him to his first show. Soon he was traveling all over the county, collecting ribbons wherever he went.

On Saturdays, Jane was allowed to take the rides out on him. She felt so proud as she sat bolt upright on the lively pony. The children following behind on their ordinary mounts would gaze in admiration at the pair.

No one else was allowed to ride Prince Brownie because he always wanted to canter whenever his hooves touched grass, and he didn't want to stop when he reached the road.

Jane would help Ruth to prepare for shows, washing Brownie and braiding his mane. He would get rather fed up with all the poking and scrubbing and would nip and kick at the pair.

Even if it was an impossible dream to ever own Prince Brownie, being able to ride him was the next best thing. Jane would help look after him and pretend that he was really hers.

But as time went on and Prince Brownie and Ruth competed at show after show, there was one thing that Jane did not realize. Ruth was getting too big for Prince Brownie. She was much older than Jane and her feet were hanging down too low beneath his belly.

On one particular cold afternoon, Jane was waiting at the stables for Prince Brownie's return from a show. As dusk began to fall, the noise of the horsetrailer brought her rushing to open the yard gate.

Once again he had returned with a ribbon and she hugged his muscular neck with pride. She had just finished double bolting his stable door, when her mother arrived to take her home.

"Before we leave," she said, "I have something for you." She handed Jane a white envelope. "When I asked Mrs. Watson if she would sell Prince Brownie, I did not think that she would agree. But Ruth really needs a bigger horse and so she said 'yes'. Inside is a receipt."

"I can't believe it!" said Jane. Her impossible dream had come true. Prince Brownie was finally hers!